Super Nonno!

By Guy Marini

Inspired by Ethan Daniel & Mackenzie Leigh

"Super Nonno!" published by Guy Marini. Copyright Guy Marini 2018. All rights reserved. All characters and their likenesses are trademarks of Guy Marini. All characters and incidents are fictional and were created entirely by Guy Marini.

Dedication:

This book is dedicated to my grandchildren, Ethan & MaKenzie. Once these two came into the world, I was transformed into a fun, loving, happy go lucky, older guy who liked nothing more than doing stuff with these two bright, beautiful and talented children. When we are together we are like that bunny on television, we just keep going and going until we are too tired to have any more fun. Our days together are filled with hugs, smiles, laughter and love. Thank you so much Ethan and MaKenzie – this book is for you!

My name is Guy.
One day I was a regular guy...
I was married, had kids, had a job, drove
a car and ate a lot of pizza...

I would get up and hug my wife... Her name
is Mrs. Guy. She likes me.

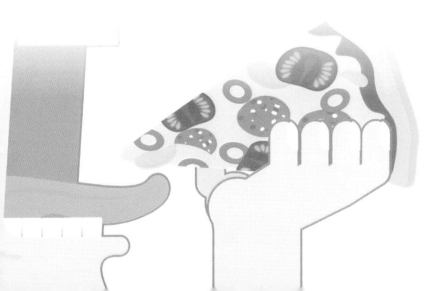

3

SIR OLIVER

I have a dog, a Morkie... 1/2 Maltese and 1/2 Yorkie... get it Morkie!
His name is Sir Oliver. We go for a walk every day.

I go to work and have meetings, talk on the phone and write reports.
A long day would end with two hugs from Mrs. Guy. She really likes me;
and, kisses from Sir Oliver - very sloppy.

Then one day, my son, Mr. Matt, called me
and said I had a grandson and a grand daughter.
Well, I was really happy and couldn't wait to meet them.

Kenzie

Ethan

Then I thought I didn't want my new little buddies to meet old boring Guy. I was a little bit sad. I went to bed that night praying and hoping that I could be somehow new and exciting.

When I woke up I noticed I was somehow wearing a cool blue
t-shirt with an American flag on it and very handsome short blue
pants. I looked at my feet and I had dazzling white sneakers on.
I hopped out of bed and looked in the mirror. A voice rang out from
the sky. "Guy... you are now changed... you are transformed...
no more boring mettings... no more hugs from Mrs. Guy, just kisses
(two cheeks)... you are now the one and only...

SUPER
NONNO!

I asked the voice what it meant to be Super Nonno. What should I do? How was my life going to change? Will my grand children like me better as Super Nonno or as Mr. Guy?

The voice said... Mr. Guy and Super Nonno were one in the same. I was now Super Nonno because I had two new little buddies who would show me how to become Super Nonno. I was confused but I said OK... I can't wait!

Well sure enough, when I met my two little buddies... Ethan and Kenzie...
I found myself transformed into Super Nonno!

I suddenly became absolutely amazed by the littlest, newest, things like
a jack in the box! I turned the handle, heard the music and couldn't
believe it when the Jack popped out. I played with Jack, Ethan, and
Kenzie for hours. After watched Jack come out of the box, I was finally
able to imitate the Jack in the box leaping out... so Ethan and Kenzie
would make believe they wound me up with my head bowed down and
I would slowly raise my head, throw my arms in the air and instead of
Jack, Super Nonno jumped up and came to life!

That was a lot of work and we were all hungry so we made a mess or uhhh... we made pancakes with faces on them. Mr. Guy had never done that but with the help of Kenzie and Ethan, Super Nonno was able to make them. Holy Cow!

After we cleaned up, we talked to Sir Oliver and he wanted to visit the zoo to say hi to his animal friends. Ethan and Kenzie said "What do you think Super Nonno?" "Do we go?" Super Nonno looked skyward and after inspecting the sun and clouds said... "Yes Sir Oliver, yes Ethan, yes Kenzie - we must see the animals."

We visited the zoo and saw lions, elephants, monkeys, otters and a big, old, rolly, polly bear. It was clear Sir Oliver was very happy as he spent time with his friends and Ethan, Kenzie and I got to learn about these animals. Sir Oliver's friends were now our new friends as we listened to the smart zoo people tell us all about what the animals ate, where they live and what they did for fun.

We were in the car coming home when Sir Oliver, Kenz, and Ethan thanked Super Nonno for a great day! I told them it wasn't over. Super Nonno had plans for the evening. The kids cheered and Sir Oliver barked happily.

Super Nonno, inspired by his three buddies, said there was only one thing to do - "Bowling!"

So there we were rolling balls down the lane, eating pizza (I like pizza), drinking juice and laughing as Sir Oliver chased the ball down the lane. He was a good bowler. He didn't need a bowling ball - he just ran down the lane and knocked the pins over.

We came home and Mrs. Guy (now known as Super Nonna) had snacks ready for us. We decided Super Nonna and Nonno would sleep in the bed while Ethan, Kenz, and Oliver would sleep in sleeping bags on the floor. We talked and laughed about our day and told Super Nonna about all the fun we had.

Soon all were asleep... Super Nonna smiled at Super Nonno and said, "You are the same Mr. Guy, but thanks to Ethan and Kenzie you are now Super Nonno." I think she was right. Do you think so?

Draw a picture of Kenzie and Ethan!

Draw a picture of your favorite zoo animal!

About The Author
Guy Marini

   Guy Marini is a businessman, author, poet, actor and the world's largest consumer of pizza. He enjoys hanging out with Mrs. Guy, Mary Lee. He walks his dog Sir Oliver everyday to keep the streets of Pawtucket, RI safe. He has 3 kids...Matt, Dani & Erika...his original buddies. He smiles a lot when he thinks about Melissa, Samantha & Danielle's mystery date.   Oh yeah, he's also the luckiest guy on planet Earth. Do you know why? He has 2 grandchildren named Ethan Daniel & Makenzie Leigh! Obviously he is also a very good friend of the Easter Bunny. Mr. Marini is also the creator of the now famous, Marini Easter Egg Hunt.